OUR BROKEN LAND

Hákon Aðalsteinsson

Published Exclusively and Globally by Far West Press

www.farwestpress.com

First Edition

ISBN 979-8-9858067-9-3

Printed in the United States of America

Hákon Aðalsteinsson is an Icelandic musician, cutting his teeth touring internationally with Singapore Sling in the mid 2000's. He has been living in Berlin for over a decade, where he has established himself as songwriter and lyricist with his own band The Third Sound.

Since 2018 he has played guitar in The Brian Jonestown Massacre and written and performed for his other projects including the country tinged Gunman and The Holy Ghost, an electronic experimental duo Diagram with drummer Fred Sunesen and the recently formed Golden Hours, a collaboration with musicians from Belgium and England.

Our Broken Land is his first Book.

--

I would like to thank Craig Dyer for editorial advice and other suggestions, Tom Giddins for copy editing and most of all I want to thank my love Lilly Creightmore for her encouragement and tremendous help making this book happen.

1.

He rarely left the house anymore. The strong sewer stench that lingered over the city was nauseating beyond comprehension, and besides, he hardly had any errands to run these days.

Occasionally, when he had grown tired of the limited delivery meal options in his area, he would get dressed and drag himself to the local supermarket. Usually, it coincided with the point in time he ran out of toilet paper.

Following his shopping trip, he would cook himself a proper meal, a Sunday roast, imitating his mother's culinary skills the best he could. Her cooking, back when she was still alive, was one of the few things he had truly enjoyed in his younger years and something he had started looking forward to as soon as the weekend began. Still now, as he prepared his own Sunday replicas, he sometimes became nostalgic, thinking of his mother and how he missed her. He even tried recreating the atmosphere by lighting candles and playing a broadcasted mass on his kitchen radio from a Christian radio station, or otherwise a recording he found online. Not that he was religious, or strictly eating these dinners only on a Sunday, they happened whichever weekday the supermarket trip fell on, but getting as close to the atmosphere of the past as possible still meant something to him. Those were the rare occasions he still felt almost human.

The view from his bedroom window over the little field at the back of the house was truly a depressing sight. The grass appeared permanently dead, never became green. It was covered in dirt and dead leaves from withered trees that resembled giant mummified hands reaching for the sky, looking for salvation. A small pond with muddy banks was located in the middle of the field and from time-to-time ducks could be seen swimming on the polluted brown water. But something was not quite right about those ducks; they sounded strange. Rather than the usual quack ducks make, it sounded more like they croaked. *When had that started?* He couldn't remember. Or maybe it had been like that ever since he moved in.

It was more than 10 years since Robert started renting that old, little house and now at the tender age of 33 it had almost become his whole existence; his universe had decreased to its interior. Time had neither a linear, nor circular structure anymore, it felt more like being held under water and only being allowed to the surface for air once in a while.

Nowadays he spent most of his time in the bedroom. Whether it was remotely programming for the evil company that paid his wages, tipping online strippers for fulfilling his sexual desires, eating or sleeping – it all happened in the bedroom. In fact, apart from the necessary trips to the bathroom down the hallway and those rare occasions he cooked and ate in the kitchen, he never stepped in any of the other rooms anymore. The rest of his own home had become foreign, like being a guest at someone else's place.

Needless to say, the state of the bedroom had steadily declined, culminating into what can only be described as absolute filth. He never cleaned, there were empty fast-food wrappers and boxes scattered around, crumpled tissues filled with crusted semen, empty cups and bottles... Robert couldn't remember the last time he changed his bedsheets and had become immune to the horrible stink in the room. He was now part of it and there was no one around to tell him.

His communication with the outside world was also on the decline. Apart from superficial interactions with online strippers or colleagues over work-related issues there wasn't much going on. He would receive a phone call from his sister every now and then but could rarely be bothered picking up. Her prying and weak attempts to establish some sort of family relationship were more than he could handle – an injection of venom straight to the heart. Her whining voice, her dumb show off husband, their loud ill-mannered and spoiled children; he felt sick even thinking about it. Which he rarely did, but he vaguely remembered the last time he spoke to her was shortly before last Christmas.

"Are you joining us for dinner over the holidays?" Her voice even more annoying than usual.

"No, I'm afraid not. Too busy...busy working."

He swallowed as he listened to her droning on about her life and some people from their past he couldn't remember anymore. When her monologue halted in a dramatic pause his heart jumped, as he knew what was about to happen.

"Have you spoken to father?" Her voice more hesitant than before.

"You know perfectly well that I haven't. There's no need to bring it up each and every time." His heart now raising, blood started boiling in his veins.

"I just miss it... being all together like a family."

At this point Robert's repressed rage had reached a point that made him unable to follow the conversation, completely zoning out. He might have given mechanical, one syllable answers to her questions, he couldn't remember, but suddenly it was all over; she had hung up. His anger deflated and he sank back in the chair where he sat feeling relieved, his hands still trembling.

They had never been close, him and his sister, and their communication was always somewhat awkward. There was a time when he bothered trying, but those days were long gone. The only person he ever truly felt close to was his mother. Her death, now almost ten years ago, was the moment in time when life lost the little meaning it had.

The relationship with his father was non-existent. He could not even stand the thought of him. From a young age, Robert had seen him as a horrible pathetic man and they had nothing in common, or so he felt at least. His parents got divorced when he was 9 years old after his dad had an affair and had consequently been violent towards his mother several times. He had treated her badly and that was something Robert would never forgive.

There had been a few occasions in the past when his father had tried reaching out, but Robert ignored it as he had sworn never to talk to him again. Now, the only memories of his father he had left were from the time they all still lived together, as he stormed off to work in an angry silence, while the rest of the family sat having breakfast.

In his late teens and early adult life Robert used to enjoy a drink, usually by himself, but had given it up years ago. The anxiety the aftermath of a drunken night brought over him had eventually become too much of a burden; shame and self-hatred of paralysing proportions. The drinking had however initially opened the door for him into the world of interacting with women, resulting in him finally getting close to one on his twenty second birthday. He was always way too shy and awkward to even try talking to anyone of the opposite sex as a teenager and even after discovering alcohol it took him a while before plucking up the courage. Like many young men he had been obsessed by the idea of sex since his early teens, but his incapability to approach girls filled him with anger and self-doubt. Although constant masturbation gave some form of relief, it also filled him with a strange sense of guilt he couldn't explain.

So finally on his twenty second birthday, after sinking a few drinks, he felt courageous enough to walk into a brothel and acquire service from a prostitute. It didn't end well though, he got too nervous as soon as they entered a private room and the built-up pressure prevented him from getting an erection. He felt too embarrassed to even look her in the eye as he handed over the money for the failed session. It took about two months before he could face going back and that time he lost his virginity. He came almost immediately, which left him with a feeling of a shallow victory; like he had not really got his money's worth.

From then on, the visits to prostitutes became a regular thing. His confidence grew along with his perverse desires to control these women. He became more and more dominant, more reckless and refused to wear condoms even though it was required. But as so often happens when flying too close to the sun, he came crashing down one day when he found out he had caught an STD. At first, he tried ignoring it, hoping it would just sort itself out somehow, but his toilet trips became so agonising that he let out a scream each time he started urinating. Robert had always hated hospitals and those sorts of institutions, but knew he had no choice. After his urine test had been examined, antibiotics were prescribed.

He felt crushed and humiliated by the whole experience and gave up visiting the brothels for good.

He completely lost all sexual desires for a few months but when they finally re-emerged, he found a new way of soothing his urges. Never being able to fully get on board with the cold mechanical atmosphere of hardcore pornography - the dead eyes breaking the fourth wall as they stared down the lens of the camera capturing them fucking in a tacky, rented vacation flat somewhere - he needed an alternative that had a slightly more human touch. When he discovered cam girl websites he felt as if his prayers had been answered. Realising he could interact with them and they would do pretty much what he demanded as long as they got paid, it felt like an arrangement he could get behind. He was in control and yet the distance gave him the option of being hidden in the shadows. It was the perfect arrangement, or so he felt for a while at least. He was of course aware that it was not real, that the young women only interacted with him for payment, but that was all the intimacy he really needed. Sometimes they chatted, sharing superficial information about how their day was going or whatever they had been up to, or Robert might even tell them that he was busy at work without explaining it further. Still, he never got deluded by the situation, thinking they were in love with him or were developing emotional bonds. He understood the dynamic of the interaction perfectly and was happy with it. Until lately.

Something was brewing in his head; something had started scratching the surface of his routine existence. Had the dull, monotone repetition finally cracked his persona? How long had this been coming?

Whatever it was, something had woken within and he wasn't content in his repeated little ways anymore. He felt irritated when he was supposed to be working, to the point he couldn't concentrate. Breaking away from programming formulas on his computer screen, pacing around the floor. He tried watching TV or even taking a bath, but nothing gave release from the growing frustration. It all seemed futile and pointless; his life was so insignificant. *Why even go on?* Robert thought to himself.

For days he struggled sleeping. Nothing seemed right anymore and there was no escape from the unidentified feeling that had taken hold of him and was shaking down his pathetic existence.

Irritation and anxiety grew stronger day by day. Irregular heartbeats, dehydration, diarrhea; It came to the point that he thought his body was failing. Although, never an athlete, or particularly health concerned, it still felt like a premature reminder of his mortality.

Then, another sleepless night, laying on his bed staring at the ceiling, everything went silent suddenly. His weight doubled and he started sinking into his mattress, struggling to breath. At first, he thought to himself: This is it, my final moment. He closed his eyes, waiting for his breath to leave him and his heart to stop. But instead, something else happened. He filled his lungs with the stale air of the bedroom, then sat up on the bed, his heart suddenly raising with excitement. He hadn't felt like this for years and was not sure at first what was happening. Was this real?

After sitting and contemplating for a moment, he realised that there was no way around it. It had to be right.

Robert had an idea.

2.

For a while he had been standing there watching, puzzled by the young man's odd behaviour. It was not like anything he had ever seen before.

Dressed in an old pair of jeans, a t-shirt and a thin summer jacket, the sweat was dripping down Robert's face. He had a few necessities with him in a backpack, but he wasn't really packed for travelling. Yet he had no intention of returning back home. Slowly he was getting used to the awful smell of sewage that hit him hard when he left his house about half an hour earlier

The sun burnt fiercely in the blue sky above him, leaving no shadows to hide in. A low electric hum could be heard from a distance; a hypnotic rumble that for some reason reminded Robert of a freezer meat locker that was about to break down. He didn't know where the idea came from, maybe something he had seen in a film or one of those nonsensical video clips that spread all over the internet like cancer these days.

After cleaning his glasses and wiping the moisture off his brow, he put them back on and kept watching the young man from a safe distance. The tall, skinny, yet muscular black fellow was acting strange, and his peculiar behavior had aroused Robert's curiosity. Pearls of perspiration were sparkling on his shaved head in the stark sunlight, even visible from where Robert stood. The young man wore a dirty shirt that looked way too big on him and his jeans were cut off by the knee. *Probably been wearing the same clothes for weeks*, Robert thought to himself. His feet were bare which must have caused discomfort on the boiling tarmac. The movements seemed erratic as he paced back and forth between a big dumpster and a pile of garbage bags that he kept organising and re-arranging into some sort of a structure. Judging by his demeanour, it was an extremely important and stressful task, a matter of life or death perhaps. Sometimes he would stop for a moment, examine his fortress of trash before yelling and cursing. Then he would attack the structure, break it down and start over whilst constantly talking to himself, or someone invisible. Robert couldn't hear quite clearly what the man was saying but suspected it was either a foreign language or a made up one. This procedure happened repeatedly, like the poor disturbed fellow was stuck in some sort of a loop and would be there trying to build his castle until the end of time. Maybe there was some logic behind it above Robert's understanding? He seriously doubted it; pure madness seemed to be at play.

The world outside Robert's home didn't look so appealing, which of course he knew, but the state of it seemed worse than he expected. There was trash everywhere, broken windows and burnt cars. Everything was deteriorating. When had it gone so wrong? How long had he been locked in his own little world, in that little house? Robert felt like he had just woken up after years of hibernation. Unless it had always been like this, without him realising, and he was now finally seeing the real world through new eyes after a moment of clarity.

Suddenly, he felt something stroking against his ankle. Startled, he jumped back, only to discover a skinny, little white cat at his feet. The cat didn't seem to be afraid and was again rubbing its head against Robert's ankle before he could move out of the way. When it started purring loudly, Robert picked it up to take a better look. It was a young male cat and it looked as if it had been on the street for some time, judging from its dirty fur and skinny appearance.

"Hey little fellow, what's your name?"

Robert was surprised by the soft, childlike tone of his own voice. That kind of talk sounded foreign coming out of his mouth. He looked around quickly, fearing someone might have heard him, but no one apart from the disturbed young man, who was busy with his own problem, could be seen. With the cat up against his chest, stroking its head, Robert started walking down the street. He could hear the young man shouting in the distance but by now Robert knew it had nothing to do with him. Although feeling sorry for the guy, there was nothing to do; the young man was beyond help it seemed. So, he left him to his own devices, labouring away and arguing with his invisible friend.

Robert had his own path to follow and was glad he had found a companion to bring along. He kept stroking the cat's head, listening to it purring in his arms. He decided to name it Sam.

There was a spring in his step as he turned down the next alleyway.

3.

The tall buildings seemed to come charging at him as he approached the city centre. The heat made him feel weak and dehydrated but he had forgotten to bring water. The cat seemed comfortable in his arms, but probably needed some food and water as well. Robert started looking around in hope of finding a place that could be of help and it was then he noticed the camp of tents on each side of the road. There were no cars around, so he walked straight down the middle of the street as he approached the camp site on the sidewalks. People were sitting in circles between the tents sharing bottles of cheap alcohol, giving him a dead stare as he passed by. From occasionally reading the news Robert knew about people's housing struggles; there were more homeless people now than ever before and things just kept getting worse. Large sums of people were losing their jobs daily and those in charge were not offering any solutions. Seeing it with his own eyes made Robert realise the situation was much worse than he possibly could have imagined. He was shocked and horrified by the misery.

Pressing Sam tighter to his chest, he started walking faster when people from the camp site approached; feeling them watching, even though he tried avoiding eye contact.

The buildings were all boarded up. The businesses in the centre of the city had closed down a while ago it seemed. Yet people still slept in tents rather than breaking in to take shelter. *Maybe they are still being guarded by security*, Robert wondered. *Some rich fuckers still own the buildings and would rather see them empty than give people a roof over their heads.* It didn't seem unlikely.

In his peripheral vision he saw a group of the campers getting closer. They moved slowly and the drowsy voices called out to him, but he struggled understanding what was being said. They were obviously after something; money, drugs, alcohol, food... probably whatever they could get. By now Robert had broken into a run as he felt their hands trying to grab hold of him, having to fend them off by pushing back whilst holding Sam with his other hand. The cold lifeless fingers seemed to be coming from everywhere, brushing against him, grabbing his clothes. Their voices unifying in a choir of miserable groans. Suddenly it was as if in a zombie apocalypse film. It felt unreal. A surreal nightmare, that takes you a while to get out of even after waking up – except here, there was no way out.

Robert kept running, now with his eyes half closed. It felt like the campsite was endless; now he was the one stuck in a loop, like the young man he had seen earlier. Running as fast as he could, he finally noticed that the tents weren't as close to each other as before. The voices became distant and in a few moments, it was all gone; there was no sign of the campsite or its residents anymore. It did not take long until he started wondering if it had only been his imagination. Finally, he stopped on a street corner, hunched over, panting. Everything was quiet.

Looking around, Robert realised he was now just outside the main city centre. The buildings were not as tall, most of them two or three storey high, and the streets seemed a little bit cleaner. It was an area that consisted of small businesses and residential flats. There were signs for bars, restaurants, hairdressers, bakeries, flower shops... but most of them out of business already and boarded up.

Still dying of thirst and worried about Sam, he searched for a corner shop or some place to buy water. A feeling of doubt took hold of him suddenly; was his decision just a moment of madness? Should he just forget the whole thing and return home? He pushed the thoughts away and kept walking down the empty street. Occasionally a car would drive by, but there were no other pedestrians around. Is this the calm before the storm, he wondered?

A narrow dark alleyway offered a momentary shelter from the sun. He sat down on the ground with his back up against the wall, feeling exhausted after all the running. He let go of Sam for the first time since he had picked him up, giving him the freedom to stretch and walk around. To Robert's surprise, Sam sat down next to him immediately and licked his paws, not showing any signs of wanting to leave. Somehow that reinforced Robert's beliefs; he had made the right decision and was there for a reason. While scratching Sam behind the ear, he slowly felt his body regaining the strength to go on.

Down at the next street corner he noticed a man stepping out of a flat-roof, one storey building with a broken neon sign above the door. Part of the sign had been removed or had fallen off so all it said was: 'ol Ha', which didn't indicate anything about the establishment. By looking at the building Robert would have assumed it was another place that had gone out of business, but the man leaving gave a strong clue of what went on inside. He was staggering down the street, blind drunk without a doubt and completely oblivious to Robert's and Sam's presence as he proceeded stumbling across the street right in front of them.

Having given up drinking about ten years earlier and not having been inside a bar for about thirteen, Robert took a moment deciding whether this was a wise move. Alcohol had been a burden in the past, but his life had not been great after he stopped drinking either.

"Come on Sam, we are both thirsty."

4.

The first thing he noticed as he entered was the smell; urine, years of tobacco smoke and something... old?

It was a bigger place than he had imagined, not a bar as he first assumed but a pool hall. Robert examined the room which was half empty. Only one pool table out of eight was occupied by two large men, with greasy hair and untrimmed facial hair. There was a bar in one corner of the square room and seven men sat there on barstools drinking.

Hesitantly he approached the bar and took a seat at the very corner up against a wall, distancing himself as much as he could from the rest of the men who sat together in a group. They all wore dirty work clothes and looked like the sort of men Robert would have avoided associating with at all costs back when he used to go out drinking. *They probably work for the city*, Robert thought, *doing manual labour of some sort*. It used to be only the desperate and the damned working these jobs back in the day, but times had changed, Robert tried reasoning.

"We are all just stuck on this sinking ship." He muttered to himself.

Feeling their eyes upon him, Robert adjusted himself on the barstool after putting Sam down on the floor next to his feet. Even without looking he knew they were observing him, talking under their breath, but strangely, given the situation, Robert kept his cool and stared blankly at the wall behind the bar table. He pretended not to notice their looks of contempt and it seemed to work, as their focus soon enough shifted back to the little TV behind the bar which was showing a football match.

A slender, older man with balding grey hair and a thick moustache stepped out from the backroom behind the bar and scanned the hall, checking how his customers were doing. Finally, he noticed Robert sitting in the corner without a drink and swiftly moved over. He had a friendly smile and nodded politely.

"What can I get you sir?"

Robert ordered a beer and asked the bartender if he had anything for Sam, darting his eyes down to the floor. The old man leaned over and lit up with joy when he noticed the cat stretching on the floor.

"I will get him some milk." He disappeared into the backroom again.

Robert discreetly studied the looks of his fellow drinkers, all of them being the same type of rough and strongly built men with permanently hardened expressions on their faces. Probably all doing road work and other types of construction jobs. *Part of the few who still have work in the real world, although anyone with a job these days should consider themselves lucky*, Robert thought to himself. Suddenly all the men let out a big groan of disappointment before cursing at the TV screen. A chance lost for their team.

The bartender returned with Robert's beer and handed him a bowl of milk, which Robert laid down on the bar table before picking Sam up and placing him in front of it. The men around the bar quickly looked in his direction again as soon as Sam started lapping up his milk, shaking their heads before returning to the game.

Robert took a big sip of his beer, the first in about ten years. It was cold and crisp, it felt as if a pleasant electric current shot down through his whole body. Robert closed his eyes, focusing on the calming feeling that traveled through him, but felt self-conscious as he was met with stares from the other patrons when he opened them again. He nervously petted Sam's back distracting himself.

The bartender who had been standing in the other corner of the bar, chatting with the workers and watching the game, now came walking over. Still with the same warm smile, he rested his elbows on the bar table in front of Robert and let out a sigh as he gazed over the pool hall.

"You know, twenty years ago when I bought this place it was full every night. Every single table occupied."

Robert nodded sympathetically as he laid the beer bottle back down on the table, his eyes firmly on the old barman who looked like he had been transported back in time as he reminisced. He broke out of it and continued:

"Now it's empty, no customers. I can't even stay open more than four nights a week."

His voice shaking at this point and Robert thought he could see the old man tearing up although his smile remained. Not being known for making small talk and despite feeling quite awkward in the situation he found himself in, Robert felt obliged to ask about his struggles. There was something so warm and genuine about the old man that Robert felt he could not let him down by any means, forcing himself to engage in a conversation. He asked if selling the place had ever occurred to him.

"Oh, they have been trying to kick us out of here for years. They wanted to buy the property to knock down the building, a big development plan for the whole area, you see. But I always said no."

Robert was still thinking of a follow up question when the old man went on:

"That's until the recession of course. When everything came to a standstill, no one cared anymore. But no customers either."

The old man laughed as he walked away to fetch more beers for the workers, who were now talking loudly amongst themselves. The game was either finished, or it was half time; none of them were watching the screen.

After a few more beers Robert felt relaxed, a light buzz from the alcohol tickling his brain. From the corner of his eye, he saw someone approaching the empty space at the bar next to him and sitting down on the barstool. Robert emptied his beer bottle before giving the newcomer a glance. To his surprise it was not another worker, but a black clad being. Their eyes met for a brief moment before Robert looked away shyly. As she searched through her handbag, Robert observed the young woman cautiously. Her straight black hair, a complete contrast to her pale white skin. Her eyebrows were drawn on her face and gave an otherworldly look. Her facial expression was completely blank, like she wasn't aware of her surroundings at all.

The bartender came over and she ordered rum and coke, which didn't seem to please him judging by his expression. Until now he only needed to hand out a beer bottles. As the bartender mixed the drink, Robert noticed the eyes of the other guests turning their direction once again. They seemed even more appalled now, looking at Robert with his cat and the weird looking goth girl at the end of the bar. *Probably just two freaks that don't belong in their world*, Robert thought.

Their eyes met again, but this time Robert didn't shy away, and they kept looking at each other until the silence between them became uncomfortable.

"What's its name?" She finally asked.

"What?"

"Your cat, what's its name?"

5.

There was something ghost-like about her, the slow movements, the monotone voice. She was totally over dressed for the heat in her long black dress and she reeked of body odour.

Robert offered her another drink, they had already shared a few, she accepted with a faint smile.

Dawn, who Robert realised wasn't her real name, yet a strange "stage name" for such a nocturnal looking creature, had told him that she was a sex worker that mainly worked as a dominatrix.

Intrigued by the idea Robert wanted to know more. He had never met a dominatrix before and felt like he was entering an unknown territory; it was terrifying yet thrilling. He had never been dominated back in the day when he used to visit prostitutes, then it was him that desired to be in control. But now the idea of someone else having power over him was stirring something up within. He had seen some of the cam girls offering the service, but through a computer screen it felt too distant and not real enough, almost ridiculous even. Her sitting there right next to him, made his fingers tremble with excitement and he forgot everything else that was going on around them. In his mind people had stopped meeting up for sexual rendezvous years ago, so it almost felt like meeting a person from the past, a time traveler of some sort.

By now the alcohol had filled him with the confidence of his younger self. Perhaps drinking again brought back the memories of when he was regularly having sex in the real world, in his early twenties, with prostitutes.

"You know, I hadn't had a drink for about ten years until today." He looked at her with half open eyes, thinking it made him look sexy.

"So why today?" Her drugged out, low energy made it hard to tell if she was even slightly interested in the conversation, or just humouring him out of politeness.

"Well, I am going through some changes. I had an epiphany let's say... it's the first day of the next chapter of my life."

"What about him?" Her eyes gazed at Sam, who was now sleeping on the bar.

"He joined me on my mission today." Robert smiled.

"Oh, so you are on a mission, are you?"

At this point Robert wasn't sure if she was mocking him.

"Well, it is hard to explain... Why don't you tell me more about yourself, about your... work?"

He was interested in knowing what happened at her sessions, what her clients asked for, whether she drew the limit somewhere, how much she charged...
She didn't seem bothered by his questions, became slightly more passionate if anything, and that pushed Robert's curiosity and confidence even further; even attempting to crack a joke or few. She laughed and stared deeply into his eyes.

"So, what brings you to this part of town? You don't look like you are from around here."

"I ended up here by chance pretty much. My mission probably led me here, maybe to meet you."

Dawn's smile was hard to read, after this pitiful, comment. Yet she remained as calm as before.

A commotion coming from the other side of the bar grabbed their attention. Two of the workers were already on their feet exchanging blows; a proper fist fight had broken out. The other men jumped up from their barstools shouting and trying to smooth things over, but the two who fought were already fully engaged and ignoring all pleas from their fellow drinkers, who now had made a half circle around them.

Robert felt a rush of adrenaline and imagined himself in an old western film. He saw the bar owner standing with his arms crossed behind his bar, calmly shaking his head.

The bigger of the two men kept lunging at the shorter one, who was quick enough on his feet to duck the heavy punches. That's how they danced around for a while, the towering fellow throwing his fists around, while the shorter and quicker one smoothly moved out of the way like a professional boxer. Finally, the big guy lost his patience and pulled out a knife. At which point the other workers stepped in between and held them back. Both men tried to break loose, but soon enough the shouting quietened and the two men calmed down, so the others let them lose. They walked up to each other, the others still on guard, and exchanged a few words.

To Robert's surprise it didn't take long until the two fighters were laughing together and patting each other on the back. Then they sat back down and clinked their beer bottles before emptying them. A few moments later they were fully embraced in each other's arms, lost in a deep conversation. The others paid no attention to them anymore, it was as if it had never happened.

Robert was puzzled by the whole scene, Dawn wasn't too bothered. The owner seemed relieved and was already serving more beer.

"I wonder what that was about." Robert looked back at Dawn.

"Probably nothing. I bet they won't even remember tomorrow. It's not so uncommon seeing those guys fighting, although this place is usually very quiet, which is why I come here."

"Are those types of guys your clientele?"

"Sometimes, but lately it is mainly people that earn more money. Everyone is so broke these days." She sucked more rum and coke through the straw in her drink.

"And how does someone as beautiful as you end up doing this type of work."

Dawn's forced smile filled Robert with shame, thinking he had gone too far, that she would stand up and leave. But she seemed to be used to these sorts of comments, maybe even far worse.

"I left home early. Me and my mother didn't get along, so I had to move out and have been living on my own ever since. And you've got to do what you can to make ends meet I suppose... you know?"

Robert nodded while staring at her, transfixed; impressed by the young woman's courage. *How old is she, twenty-two or three maybe?* Robert wondered.

"So, you only do it for the money then, you don't enjoy it?"

"Sometimes I enjoy it, it depends on the sub and each situation… I guess I wouldn't do it if I didn't have to." She shrugged her shoulders.

"And you say that they usually don't even want to have sex with you…"

Looking up at the ceiling she sighed and shook her head before a devious smile appeared on her face.

"I'm sorry if I am asking too many questions, it is just something I am curious about as I have never met a dominatrix before." Robert looked at her apologetically.

"Look, if you really want to know what goes on in my sessions, it is easy enough for you to find out."

"How do you mean?"

"I could just show you. If you are up for trying it out?"

"What here?"

"My place is five minutes away."

He stared at her, his eyes wide open. His mouth opened next, but words refused to come out. Dawn grinned back at him seductively as she moved her head back, throwing her long black hair over her shoulder.

"You can bring Sam; I've got some food for him."

6.

It felt like a trip to hell, a darkened netherworld where one could access past lifetimes and see into the future simultaneously; intertwined timelines all at once. Where truth could be found and lost during the same split second. Spastic and abstract jump cuts between dimensions, revealing a second of beauty before a lifetime of terror would fade into a new scene that was familiar but didn't quite make sense. Zoning in and out, not knowing where or what you are. So terribly funny and yet so strange and scary that there is no way of getting your head around it. The threads, those links, how it all comes together and how easily it all crumbles to pieces again, leaving nothing, no memory or revelation.

The demonic voices kept whispering, he couldn't get them to stop. At the same time, it was as if someone was trying to tell him something important through a broken radio, but he could never really grasp the meaning. Things were either moving too fast or too slowly, he went six times around the world in the blink of an eye but was then stuck in a pre-historic period for centuries. He felt like he had lost all control, like someone was toying with his mind.

Robert opened his eyes, still feeling disorientated and not really knowing where he was. She was standing over him, where he lay on the floor, his head centered between her legs – her high heels at ear level each side. She was naked apart from the shoes, a leather bra and a spiked dog collar around her neck. In her right hand she held a whip.

It came as a great shock to his foggy mind when the stream started gushing from her, bright and yellow, warm, and powerful, it had Robert gasping for air while splashing in his face. Jerking his head from side to side he tried pleading with her:

"St...st...op...stop...this...stop...this is...please..."

But she kept on going, the stream of urine just getting stronger. It went on for what felt like ages, soaking his twitching face.

"Stop it! This is not for me!" Robert finally managed to shout as he lifted his upper body from the ground, sat up and pushed her away.

Dawn stumbled backwards on her high heels before crashing into the coffee table behind her and falling over, landing on her butt at the other end of the room. Robert quickly got to his feet, rubbing his face with the palm of his hand. She was looking at him, startled, from the floor where she still remained, then anger took over her face, moving in like a dark cloud. She jumped to her feet and came charging at him.

"Get the fuck out of here, you fucking pervert... fucking loser!"

Completely naked, Robert started backing away. Dawn picked up his clothes from the floor and threw them at him. He fended off his garments whilst he kept backing towards the door that he had noticed behind him. With nothing left to throw she fiercely came for him, her arms like windmill sails as she attacked.

Despite her punches he managed to stumble to the front door of the apartment and get out, ending up stark naked on the sidewalk of the dark, empty street. She immediately slammed the door shut.

Robert looked around but there was no one to be

seen. Not knowing what to do, he took off his glasses and tried wiping the urine off them with his thumbs. A moment later the door opened and his clothes and shoes came flying out before it shut again.

Embarrassed and confused, he dressed in a hurry hoping no one would pass by, then started stumbling down the street. What had happened? He tried piecing together the mosaic fragments in his mind, feeling that his head was getting a little bit clearer than before.

As they had arrived at her small, messy apartment she had offered him a drug to take the edge off, as she had put it. Ketamine: a drug Robert knew only by name and was not at all familiar with. As a matter of fact, Robert wasn't much of an expert on any type of drugs, as he had never tried anything stronger than alcohol, but through popular culture and reading articles online he had an idea of the effects some of them caused, but ketamine was not one of those. He had however thought, in the spirit of his new way of thinking and as a part of his so-called mission, trying a new kind of high might be a good step for him - seeing the world with different eyes - and besides, how bad could it be? Weren't people doing drugs all the time? He was not, however, prepared for what followed, although he had enjoyed the slight dizziness and the euphoric sensation in the beginning. Soon it had become too much, to the degree that he lost all sense of self and his surroundings. It felt like being trapped in a portal connecting different universes, giving him a glimpse into each one, all at once, creating a new distorted, discord universe of its own. Nothing had made sense, yet it had felt as if messages were being passed on to him, like he had seen into the future. But now, as he walked down the darkened street, he couldn't quite remember those messages, or make any sense of the experience.

The temperature had dropped significantly and it was getting windy. Those quick shifts in the weather weren't uncommon these days, but Robert seldom experienced them spending most of his time indoors. Shivering, he had picked up his pace without realising.

"Shit!" Robert exclaimed out loud as he stopped in his tracks. Sam, he had forgotten Sam... and his backpack. For a moment he contemplated whether to return, but facing that crazy woman again was more than he could handle at that point and he decided against it. *Hopefully she will treat Sam better than she treated me*, Robert thought. Luckily, his wallet and phone were in the pocket of his jeans, so he was still connected to the world, both the real one and the digital world he was trying to escape.

Lost in his thoughts he wandered down the desolate, windy streets, still trying to make it all add up. Was he going mad? Or was he finally on to something that gave his life a sense of purpose? Robert wasn't sure, but felt he was already in too deep not to follow through. He needed to find out what awaited at the end of his journey.

When he finally became aware of his surroundings again, he realised he had stumbled into a street with bright neon lights, nightlife and pubs. He noticed drunk people all around, shouting, laughing and crying. Glass broke behind him. He had to jump into the street to avoid stepping into vomit gloriously splattered all over the sidewalk on a street corner, nearly being run over by a car in the process.

"Hey, watch it asshole!"

The aggravation came from every direction, no place to hide. Robert was amazed he hadn't noticed entering the party district until he was right in the thick of it. He felt as if he was still flickering between dimensions. He needed to get out of there.

"You got a cigarette?"

The harsh tone of the voice was startling, Robert involuntarily looked over his shoulder at the red faced, angry skinhead that stared at him with a crazy glare in his eyes. Robert hurried down the street, but the man followed.

"Hey, I'm talking to you, you fucking cunt."

He felt the man's fat fingers grabbing his arm and realised he wasn't going to escape by running away.

"Sorry, I don't smoke." Robert looked at the angry, bald man, who was obviously drunk out of his mind, apologetically.

"Oh, fuck off!"

Again, Robert's view swiftly changed, now seeing the world horizontally from the ground. It happened so fast that it took him a moment to realise that the angry skinhead had knocked him down with a punch; striking him right on the lips, and he felt them swelling already. The man stood cussing above him, but Robert was too shook up to understand what was being said. After lying motionless, watching the man's dirty leather boots shuffling around in front of his eyes for a minute, he finally saw them disappear into the night. There were people all around that he could hear talking, but no one came to help him; no one seemed to care.

He managed to drag himself up to his feet. The street was still busy with drunk people everywhere and the wind was blowing even harder now. Shivering,

Robert looked around.

"I've got to get out of here," the words repeating like a mantra from his trembling lips.

After walking for a few minutes, he saw the sign of a hotel and tried booking a room but was told that they were already full. The same thing happened at the next hotel, and the one after that. Robert started suspecting it was his appearance - a swollen lip, dirty clothes, no luggage - that was the cause rather than there being no single vacant room. He was running out of ideas.

As he came to the end of these mean streets, he spotted an old stone church in a dimly lit area close by and wondered if it could be his shelter for the night. With nothing to lose he stumbled on and felt a soothing calm come over him as the drunk street noises faded away.

He entered the cemetery surrounding the church. The trees were shielding him from the wind and the streetlights. The main door didn't open, it was thoroughly locked. Disappointed, Robert walked around the church to see if there was a back entrance, or a window he could crawl through. Quickly after it became clear there was no chance of entering, he spotted a wooden bench in the cemetery between two headstones under one of the church walls. He had never slept rough before, but at this point it seemed his best option.

Laying down to rest on the bench, he heard the faint noises in the distance. He closed his eyes and could only hope none of the drunken idiots would wander into the graveyard and harass him. By now it was freezing, Robert's teeth were chattering as he held his hands tight up to his body trying to stay warm. This wasn't what he had in mind when he left the house that morning.

7.

The organ is playing a requiem. The heavy, draconian sound reverberating in the empty church hall, making Robert's body tremble from the inside and the hair stand on the back of his neck. Although oppressive and sad, he thinks that it is the most beautiful music he has ever heard. The lights fade and the church suddenly seems like it is about to collapse, a sense of doom in the air.

"Judgement is upon us," someone whispers in his ear.

Tears start streaming down Robert's face. His mother, who is sitting by his side on the front bench, doesn't seem to notice him as she stares blankly at the altar in front of them. Never blinking, it is hard to tell whether she is conscious, or even breathing.

The altarpiece shows Jesus on the cross, crying tears of blood. Three of the apostilles are kneeling and licking Jesus' feet. The wolfish look on their faces is inappropriate, Robert finds. He tries to guess which three apostilles they are but can't remember any of their names.

He turns around and sees that all the other benches in the church are empty; no one is to be seen apart from his mother. Reaching for her hand, there is no response; it feels ice cold. Still transfixed on the altar, she starts singing along to the organ music, although her lips don't move. At first, he can't hear or understand what is being sung but she repeats the same thing over and over. He sits and listens for a while, amazed he never knew how well his mother sings. Then slowly the words become clear:

"I want to tell you something, I know it all means nothing... we dissolve into dust, never going back home to the promised land."

He has no idea what the words mean but they sound strangely familiar. The organ music is interrupted by a loud bang when the church doors are flung open. The wind is howling outside as someone walks in. The doors bang shut. The steps are echoing, as someone walks down the church aisle. Robert is too afraid to look around, his mother stops singing.

When he looks back at the altarpiece it has changed completely. The image is distorted in the half-darkness of the church, but peering at it, Robert is convinced that Jesus has gotten down from the cross and is now standing there, pointing his finger straight at him with a menacing grin on his face. The apostilles are all lying dead at his feet.

The organ stops playing as the footsteps move closer, until someone is standing next to their bench. Robert finally looks over his shoulder and meets his father's angry gaze. He is wearing a light brown suit and a trench coat, holding a suitcase in his hand; just as he dressed every day to go to work when Robert was little. He is soaking wet and has left a trail of water on the church floor. His skin is whiter than snow and there is something missing from his expression that used to be there.

"He drowned and now he is back for you," the voice in Robert's head tells him.

Robert feels his heart jump and has trouble breathing. His father steps towards them, fixes his tie and clears his throat:

"Come on now, pick your mother up and carry her

to the car.”

Robert turns to his mother who, he sees now, is silently crying; the tears dripping on her black dress.

“But I am just a boy.”

Frightened and confused, Robert looks around the church. There must be someone else there, someone that can help him. Where did that organist go?

“I am not telling you again. Do as I say, or you will regret it.” His father is trembling with anger, his jaw clenched. Pointing towards the altar, at a white coffin:

“Now pick up your mother and carry her to the car.”

Robert starts crying as he realises his mother is no longer sitting beside him and doesn’t understand how he is supposed to carry the coffin all by himself.

“But I am only nine!”

His father is livid and makes a growling sound as he nervously shuffles his feet in front of the bench where Robert sits.

“You will never amount to anything, you have always been weak and lazy.”

He reaches forward and grabs the collar of Robert’s shirt. His other hand clenched in a fist above his head.

“No please, dad. Please don’t!”

Their eyes meet and Robert is scared stiff seeing

all the anger and hatred that lives behind his father's eyes.

"There is nothing else there, it was always pure hate that fueled him." The voice is back again.

Now he understands everything, where all his fear and doubt were born. He never had a choice; it was already laid out from the day he entered the world. He feels completely vanquished, but at the same time a great sense of relief, like he can finally leave everything behind.

-

Robert woke up at first light, feeling dreadful. Shivering cold, he struggled sitting up on the bench and the strong metallic taste of blood in his mouth made him retch. He felt a throbbing heartbeat in his swollen lips and was in the grip of a hangover from hell.

"I must never do this again," Robert whispered to himself.

His body was stiff and aching when he finally managed to rise from the wooden bench, almost collapsing as he got to his feet. His legs completely numb. By now the wind had brewed into a raging storm and to make things worse, it was also raining sideways. Even the trees struggled to stay in place.

Robert managed to limp up to the church where he took momentary shelter catching his breath. He noticed a shovel standing up against the church wall and knew he would need one when he would get to his destination. No one is going to miss it.

Feeling alone and vulnerable, he tried grasping the

situation. It was like watching the world being torn apart, but maybe that was needed before any actual change was to come; the same could be said about his own life perhaps

8.

He felt it was time to leave, having already spent too much time in the city, which he now realised was rotten to the core. The only way was to keep on moving and get the fuck out of there.

With the strong wind blowing his direction, it took all his energy making his way back towards the city centre, taking regular stops in alleyways, to catch his breath and regain strength. He had to duck pieces of garbage that came flying; bottles, plastic bags, junk food wrappers... it felt like taking part in one of those ridiculous TV reality game shows that promise poor people cash prices in return for whatever little is left of their dignity, which in most cases only ended up in further humiliation.

When he reached the camp site in the centre again the atmosphere had changed drastically; people were working as a team securing their tents with rocks and tying them together. Those same creatures that yesterday had drifted around like zombies were now moving fast in unison, shouting, and trying to help each other in an adrenaline infused state of panic. They paid no attention to Robert as he passed by, but seeing their effort gave him a hint of hope for humanity, which he had come so close to giving up on. *Maybe we are not doomed after all*, he wondered as he kept marching against the wind.

It surprised him how busy the bus station was when he finally got there after what felt like an endless trek. People were running around like headless chickens, screaming and shouting; total chaos filling the air. He needed to sit down but every single bench seat was occupied, so he decided to find something to eat, as it occurred to him that it was more than twenty-four hours since he last ate.

Announcements were booming from the broken loudspeaker system, completely impossible to understand, as he tried passing through the sea of people on his way to the station's café. He started feeling faint and disorientated, his vision became blurred. No food and bad sleep were catching up with him. For a moment he thought he recognised the voice from the loudspeaker as his father's but quickly realised that was impossible. His state of confusion was only to blame.

When he finally reached the café, he was greeted by another busy room and a long queue, that seemed to move so slowly it made time pass backwards. The whole time he stood there he battled staying conscious, trying to convince himself that everything would be better once he had some nourishment in his body. The chatter all around felt like it was directed at him, that all these people were either talking at, or about him, which made him weary and paranoid. He couldn't make out the words and he knew it was only his mind playing tricks, but it felt like being under attack none the less.

"Just got to keep it together until you get to the counter," his inner voice said.

A bony teenage boy with glasses and a red cap greeted him at the end of the queue.

"What can I get you sir?"

Robert tried ordering a coffee and a sandwich, but was informed that they were all out of food apart from salted, dry biscuits.

"It's because of the weather sir, they haven't been able to bring in today's delivery."

Luckily a table had freed up just as he was handed his order, which he jumped on, beating a fat woman with an even fatter child, to it. Robert pretended not to notice them.

As he snacked on his biscuits and drank the sugar filled black coffee, that made him feel slightly better, he noticed a young family of three on a table nearby. The daughter, who Robert guessed was four or five years old, was asking why Charlie had not been able to come along.

"Aunt Rose will take good care of him darling. And besides, we are only away for a couple of weeks." Her father said in an assuring tone.

"It will go by so fast you will hardly notice, and you will be playing with Charlie again before you know it," her mother added.

"But I want to play with him now." The young girl was on the verge of tears.

Her mother gently stroked the little girl's curly hair as she glanced over to the father with a look that seemed to say: I told you so.

The discussion about Charlie, which Robert assumed was either a cat or a dog, filled him with guilt and remorse. *Should I have gone back for Sam? Was it cowardly and selfish of me to leave him there?* He knew it was pointless to wallow in these thoughts, yet it was hard to push them away. Somehow it felt like a distant memory now, or even a dream. Like that woman was just a fabrication of his imagination. *If only that was the case.*

As a child he had always been fond of animals although he had never been allowed to keep a pet. When his father lived with them, he had been dead against bringing a pet into the household, as he hated them. After he left, his mother struggled enough taking care of Robert and his sister, too much to even consider keeping a pet. Plus, there was no money.

Somehow as he got older, Robert's interest in animals faded away like so many other beliefs and feelings he used to have. His personality had slowly been peeled away, layer by layer, leaving nothing but the mere basics of human emotions. If it could even be considered human. How had it happened? Why had it been getting worse through the years? Leaving him as interesting as an empty shell. What a bleak and sad state of affairs his life had become. *But now it is all about to change*, he tried to reassure himself. Finishing his last sip of coffee, he stood up, grabbed his shovel and marched out of the café. He held his head high, carrying the shovel on his shoulder like a soldier would carry a rifle.

His spirit dropped momentarily again when he reached the enormous ticket queue. Reluctantly he joined it, feeling like he was persistently being punished. But soon enough the energy that he felt running through his veins earlier returned and convinced him he could pass every hurdle on the way. He had not felt this level of excitement for years, something was genuinely pushing him forward and giving him the strength to carry on. It was so refreshing and reassuring, like he was waltzing with a beautiful woman while gracefully moving along in the ticket queue. Nothing was going to stop him.

"I am sorry sir, but there are no more buses leaving today. All the roads out of the city have been closed because of the storm."

Robert stared at the young woman in the ticket booth behind a glass, his mouth half open in disbelief.

Her dead eyes stared back, almost through him, as she slowly chewed her gum.

No matter what he said, her expression did not change. It felt too disheartening just to give up right there and then.

"But I have to get to the cemetery, my mother..."

It was hopeless. She probably wasn't even listening, maybe immune after delivering disappointing news to thousands of would-be travelers that morning. She still had that blank look on her face and chewed the gum in the same irritating way as Robert turned away.

"Fuck this!" Robert said to himself as he stormed toward the station's exit.

He looked around and saw a taxi parked close by. The mighty wind made it difficult to walk those few steps, but when he got there, he opened the backdoor, threw the shovel on the seat, then flung himself in without checking if the cab was free. Luckily it was.

"There's no way man, they weren't lying. All the roads leading out of the city are closed," the driver said, looking over his shoulder

Rearranging himself in the back seat, not knowing what to do, Robert's frustration washed back over him with full force. The taxi driver combed his greasy, black hair while keeping an eye on Robert, waiting for instructions. After an awkward moment of silence, Robert cleared his throat:

"Take me as far west as you can. I need a place where I can get food and a bed until the storm is over." Robert's voice was firm, almost demanding.

"You got it, sir." The taxi driver started his engine without hesitation.

Rainwater was already flowing down the steep streets like rivers. The driver was cautious and drove slowly through the city in fear of being blown off the road at any moment. It was an old car that made rattling and screeching sounds as it wobbled down the windy streets, making Robert wonder if this might be its last voyage.

Passing a group of homeless people trying to take shelter under a bridge, the cab driver tutted:

"Look at those bums. It didn't used to be like this, you know. Fucking leeches of society...a fucking disgrace."

Robert decided to bite his tongue rather than engaging in a conversation that might lead to an argument. He wanted to tell the driver that the people on the street were not to blame for the fact that the threads of society were becoming undone. He wanted to tell him that pointing a finger at the homeless was finding an easy scapegoat and totally missing the point - If he wanted to find the actual root of the problem, he would have to dig deeper, and we would all have to share the blame of why society had failed. The greed and short-sighted thinking of people in charge and anyone who found the slightest bit of personal gain, was something that really had to be taken into account. He wanted to tell the taxi driver he was a fucking idiot who had no idea what he was talking about.

True, Robert had been fearful of the homeless as he passed through the camp site yesterday, but not once had the thought occurred to him of blaming them for how bad things were. And this morning seeing them working together had filled him with some sort of hope. Was it a sign of his humanity returning? He didn't know, but maybe he wasn't completely dead inside after all.

He desperately wanted to get out of the city and had no desire to leave the cab and search for another; the weather seemed to be reaching a life-threatening status at this point.

So instead of starting an argument, Robert asked the driver if he would kindly turn on the radio.

"Nah man, it's all gone."

"What do you mean?"

"Most of the stations went bust a while ago. There is no money in it anymore… and now with this weather, it's completely dead" The driver banged the car radio with his fist as if to prove his point.

"I guess that's the fault of the homeless as well?" Robert had no idea where his newfound courage came from.

"What?" The driver shot daggers of rage at Robert through the rearview mirror before mumbling something under his breath.

Robert didn't care, he felt quite pleased with himself. They drove on in silence, listening to the howling wind and the rattling noise from the car, which felt as though it could give up at any moment.

The driver smelt awfully bad, a mixture of sour sweat caused by an unhealthy diet and stale cigarette smoke. Robert felt sorry for the man as he now realised how many people lived a life that was far worse than his own. The self-confidence was returning, maybe he was on to something after all.

9.

"Well, that's as far as I'll go."

The taxi pulled up in front of an old two storey house, a black timber framed building with scarred white plaster walls.

"I know the innkeeper here, he's a decent fellow. He does good food and the rooms are cheap. He'll sort you out," the driver continued without even looking at Robert.

Despite not liking the taxi driver at all, Robert left a generous tip, which transformed the driver's attitude completely. His eyes lit up and his whole demeanour became unpleasantly friendly and apologetic, as if he now regretted the frosty response to Robert's earlier remarks. He even went so far as getting off his ass and opening the door for Robert, and then waved him off with a fake smile painted on his face while the wild wind messed up his greasy hair.

Robert disappeared through the arch entrance leading from the street into the courtyard. He found the whole experience quite amusing, chuckling to himself as he opened the inn's front door.

Warm, thick air, full of dust and a musky smell greeted him as he entered. The dimly lit, old wooden interior was a welcoming shelter from the howling storm and the whole building was creaking as he slowly walked up to the unmanned reception desk.

After standing there for a moment, leaning on his shovel, looking around, he rang the bell on top of the desk. A balding, round head popped out from the entrance to the room on Robert's right side.

"Yes, hello, please?"

The man's funny accent and cartoonish voice made Robert smile.

"I am looking for a room tonight and a bite to eat." Robert felt he was finally in a safe place after the struggles the morning had brought.

"Yes, of course." The little round man advanced forward, taking position on the other side of the reception desk.

"You are the only guest right now, I'll give you my very best room." He looked up at Robert with a big smile on his face.

Robert nodded in a grateful manner.

"Is this your only luggage?" The little man pointed at the shovel before bursting into laughter.

After completing the transaction, the man, called Claudio, led Robert through to the adjoined pub area, pulled out a chair for him at a table in the middle of the room and waited for Robert to sit down. The pub was decorated with taxidermy heads of various animals, old street signs, beakers and jugs. A wood burner was blazing away in the corner of the room; a sight Robert had not seen for years.

"My wife is sick so today I work alone. It will be a moment, but just sit down and relax."

Robert ordered a beer when Claudio returned to bring the menu over. A mellow jazz record was playing in the background and Robert felt a calm come over him as he took the first sip of his beer. It was comforting to have the place to himself and feeling the warmth generated by the wood burner, that helped drying his wet clothes.

Noises came from the kitchen where Claudio was busy preparing the food, it sounded as if he was in a state of panic.

Robert leaned back in his chair closing his eyes, finally feeling quite content. His worries and frustration were slowly melting away; this was it, what he had been waiting for.

And then for the first time since he was a child, he felt like talking to his sister. He took the phone out of his pocket and stared at it for a moment, thinking it over. Was it a good idea? Wasn't it his obligation at this point? Probably he would not speak to her again he realised.

Robert hesitated as he heard her fragile voice on the other end of the line.

"Hello, it's me...Robert," he finally said.

"Oh dear, Robert, how are you?" Her excitement sounded genuine.

"I am good... really good."

The conversation led them down a familiar path, except now it was him asking the questions about her children, her husband and how she was doing. She answered politely and without boring him with too many details.

"I quit my job," he finally said after she shifted the focus back to him.

"Oh my, did something come up?" She asked after

a slight hesitation.

"No, I just realised it wasn't doing me any good anymore... or maybe it never was."

There was a crackling sound on the line while they both remained silent.

"And what will you do?" She finally asked.

"I have things cooking, some ideas I can't say too much about right now."

"Well, that's exciting." She tried her best to sound encouraging, although it was obvious from her tone that she worried.

"And you know what, I have decided to give dad a call." He hurried to add, in an attempt to rid her of her concerns.

"What, really?" Oh, that's wonderful. I always knew you would find each other again one day." She sounded happy, which pleased Robert, even if he wasn't entirely sure why.

"Yeah, we shall see."

"So, when are you going to call him?"

Her excitement reminded Robert of how she acted at Christmas as a child and the bittersweet memory brought tears to his eyes.

"Right now, after I hang up on you."

They both laughed. He was ticking all the right

boxes and could hear that she also was on the verge of joyous tears. They went on speaking for a few more minutes and before bidding goodbye, she invited him for dinner which he accepted, although telling her they would have to decide the date another time.

He hung up, stared at the screen of the phone in his hand until it went black; It died, out of battery. Robert sighed and laid the phone on the table. He never intended to call his father, but now he had a perfect excuse and a clean conscience.

Claudio came storming out of the kitchen with Robert's meal neatly prepared on a tray which he carried carefully over to the table. The beads of sweat on his brow indicated that the cooking had been a big task for him.

"Here we are sir, pork chops, roasted potatoes and a side salad." Claudio had a frozen, nervous smile on his face as he laid the food on the table in front of Robert.

"Thank you." Robert nodded and smiled back

"Another beer sir?"

"Yeah, why not... and why don't you join me for a drink since there is no one else here?"

Claudio was caught off guard, not expecting the invitation. He wiped the sweat off his forehead, shooting his eyes from one side to the other, before a sly smile broke out on his round face.

"Yes, I will do, I will do."

Still chuckling to himself, Claudio disappeared behind the bar. Robert tucked into his food immediately, the smell reminding him of how hungry he really was; having almost forgotten.

He was halfway through wolfing down the food from his plate when Claudio returned with two beers.

"Ah, big appetite, I like!" Claudio was beaming as he sat down opposite Robert, handing him one of the beers.

"Cheers!"

"So, how long have you had this place?" Robert asked between bites.

Shaking his head, Claudio leaned forward and placed a hand under his chin. The question seemed to bring him a great deal of worry, staring into the void, before looking up and meeting Robert's eyes.

"A few years. If only I had known everything was going to shit."

Robert nodded sympathetically, still chewing on his food. Claudio's singsong accent was making it hard for him to keep a serious face and he had to clench his jaw to stop himself from grinning. He hurried to take another bite, to hide his expression.

"Yes, no people with money these days, only a few guests every month." He sighed heavily.

"It must be tough."

"Well, let's not talk about sad things... what brings you here?" Claudio snapped out of his gloom, as if he suddenly remembered his role serving his customer in the best way possible, no matter what.

"I need to get out of the city. I have some unfinished business to take care of..."

"You are a businessman?" Claudio nodded as to indicate he understood.

"No, no, not like that. It's a personal thing." Robert wiped his mouth with a napkin, having finished his last bite.

"Ah, I see... or maybe you go dig for treasure with your spade?" Claudio mimicked digging with a shovel before he started laughing.

Robert smiled back.

"But now I am stuck here until the weather allows me to leave. So, I guess we have time for a few more drinks." They both laughed before clinking their beer glasses.

"Cheers!"

Claudio stood up, an excited look on his face as he asked Robert to wait a moment, then ran behind the bar again. Robert felt full and satisfied after the meal and the beer was creating a mild buzz in his head, washing away all memories of the hangover from that morning.

Claudio returned at speed with a bottle of grappa and two shot glasses. When the glasses had been filled to the brim, the two men looked each other in the eye before clinking glasses once again:

"Tonight we drink."

A few hours later the two men were in good spirits, chatting away about everything and nothing, telling stories and enjoying each other's company. The grappa bottle now half gone and pint glasses piling up on the table. The wind kept howling, rain beating on the windows, and it was starting to get dark.

The front door in the reception hall opened abruptly. A draught blew out the candle that was a light on the table and they shuddered as the cold air from outside reached them.

"Who is there?" Claudio stretched his neck out as if it would allow him to see around the corner into the other room.

The front door closed. Keeping their eyes on the entrance to the bar, they waited in anticipation as footsteps came closer. As a young, skinny man, wearing a soaking wet trench coat, walked in, Claudio was quick to his feet.

"Oh no!" Claudio shouted.

The scruffy looking young man, with his long black hair and thick beard, was still looking around as Claudio ran towards him. He greeted Robert with a nod just before Claudio reached him and tried pushing him back out from where he had entered.

The two men started shouting at each other in their native language, waving their hands around, in what to Robert seemed like a furious argument. Claudio's head only reached up to the young man's shoulder, but he was completely fearless as the argument escalated and the two men started to push each other's chests whilst shouting.

Robert had no idea what was going on, but felt it was his duty to step in and try to calm them down.

He managed to get between the two men and slowly their anger deflated. They finally agreed to sit down and talk it over.

Claudio explained that the young man was his son, Fabio, and was there once again asking for money.

"He spend everything on wine, drugs and gamble. A complete stupid!" His contempt was obvious despite his bad choice of words.

Claudio's tone had changed, he was now talking like a figure of authority, completely ignoring Fabio's presence. The young man's fixed stare on his father seemed to say that he did not give a fuck about anything that was being said, or anything at all for that matter.

"I don't have the money. Business is bad and my wife is sick... so many hospital bills." Claudio's tone changed once again, as he now played the victim.

Robert begged him to stop and to take a deep breath. The scenario was starting to irritate him, but at the same time, he felt sorry for Claudio. The situation reminded him of when he had nursed his mother on her deathbed for weeks before she passed.

"Listen, we can sort this out. There's no need to panic." Alternating, he looked at the two men reassuringly.

"Now, how much do I owe you for my lunch? Let's sort that out first... go grab your card machine." Robert ordered rather than asked.

Claudio obeyed immediately. Robert, finding his new role surprisingly pleasing, measured up the young man who sat silently beside him looking down at the table.

"How much money do you need?" Their eyes met.

"Well, not so much... maybe..."

Claudio's angry look as he returned with the card machine silenced Fabio again. Robert was amused to discover that Fabio's accent was very similar to his father's. When he saw the amount Robert tipped, Claudio could hardly believe his eyes. Not knowing what to do with himself he shifted his weight from one foot to the other in front of the table.

"Thank you, thank you mister."

With a gesture Robert begged him to sit back down, almost resembling a mafia boss at this point.

"Now Fabio, if you can handle going back out walking through the storm to the next cash machine, I will give you my card and you can take out the amount that the daily allowance lets you. Ok?"

"Don't do it mister. You will never see him again. I know this little shit." Claudio shook his head, trying to warn Robert it was a bad idea.

"It's fine. If he doesn't come back, I will make a call and cancel the card, so the money he gets today will be the only thing on offer. However, if he returns there will be something more in it for him tomorrow." Robert shifted his focus over to Fabio again.

"So, Fabio, do you understand, and can I trust you are coming back?"

Fabio nodded.

"Yes, you can trust me." Fabio's smile was anything but convincing.

"Very well." Robert handed Fabio his card and gave him the pin number.

The young man was out the door within seconds.

-

Night had fallen and the storm was still roaring outside the window. The three men were dancing, each one on a different table, completely annihilated after drinking three bottles of grappa and countless pints of beer.

After Fabio returned, Robert had split the cash equally between father and son, who were astounded by his generosity. When Fabio tried returning the card, Robert asked him to hold on to it and told him to do the same thing the next day after the daily limit had been restored. Fabio smiled, placing the card in the inside pocket of his jacket.

Despite his father's protest, Fabio insisted on contacting a coke dealer that initially had promised to come by, but at this point did not answer messages anymore. *Probably not worth risking your life in this weather for the sake of a gram or two*, Robert had thought to himself. Instead, they just went all in with the alcohol, drinking harder than Robert had ever done before.

They danced on the tables, to music Fabio had selected, like there was no tomorrow. And perhaps there wasn't, the storm showed no signs of giving up.

Robert 33, and Claudio 45, had no understanding

of the so-called music Fabio insisted on playing. For them the electronic bleeps and the doomy repetitive rhythms could hardly be classified as music, but it didn't matter. This was their moment, and nothing would prevent them from enjoying it. A clash of cultures, a clash of generations, the three men had risen above it all in their drunken stupor.

10.

His mouth was so dry that the sandpaper like tongue was stuck to his hard palate. He did not even dare trying to open his eyes, already aware of the headache that was about to hit him.

Where am I again? Still trying to puzzle the pieces together, trying to figure out how he ended up in this state.

Slowly, the memories from last night's crazy drunkenness came washing over him like a warm ocean wave, bringing a smile to his face.

Finally, Robert opens his eyes and realises he is lying on the floor of the pub. He can hear the two men snoring in close proximity, playing second and third fiddle to the wind that still howls outside.

Eventually he manages to get on his feet and sees what state the pub is in: like it has been hit by an airstrike. Broken glass everywhere, chairs lying on their side, full ashtrays that have spilled over... Robert staggers around feeling confused and fuzzy.

The two men are sleeping in their chairs, resting their heads on the same table, still snoring in synchronicity; like father like son. Robert suddenly remembers thinking last night that maybe Claudio wasn't his real father because of how different they look, but of course he did not raise the question. Or if he did, he can't remember.

What surprises Robert the most though, is that he is topless, and his t-shirt and jacket are nowhere to be seen. Claudio and Fabio are both fully clothed which makes him wonder if this was some sort of a prank they played on him after he passed out; removing his clothes and hiding them. Or had he just felt so liberated last night that he had gone topless in some form of self-expression? That wasn't something he had ever done before, so it seemed unlikely. At least he had no recollection of doing so and it felt too much to get his head around right now.

Looking out a window he sees the trees swaying in the storm that is clearly still going strong. He realises that there is no way the roads have been opened yet, he is still stuck in this godforsaken city.

"What should I do?" He whispers to himself, while watching the trees and their battle with the wind.

Suddenly he has this strange feeling that the city itself is preventing him from leaving, like it has a mind of its own. He sits down at one of the tables that is holding several pint glasses, half empty with beer. He grabs one of them and takes a big sip, but immediately spits it back out, realising he was about to swallow a cigarette butt that was floating in the glass.

For a while he just sits there motionless, contemplating his next move, until suddenly he straightens in his seat with wide open eyes, like If the gods just breathed new life into him. Nothing was going to stop him, not even nature or the heavy, oppressive spirit of the city. And if his original plan was doomed, it only meant he would have to adapt.

The energy now brewing inside him, he gets up to his feet and paces around as the thoughts already stirred up are settling into a solid plan in his reinvigorated mind.

"Of course, it is so obvious. How did I not see it before?" His state is borderline manic at this point.

He is standing behind the bar when he becomes aware of himself again. He immediately pours himself a vodka shot, downs it and has another straight away. The alcohol warms up his insides and he inhales deeply as he commences taking off the rest of his clothes, feeling more alive than ever before.

The clock in the reception hall indicates that it is ten in the morning and Robert stops as he reaches the front door and has a quick look over his shoulder, saying a last goodbye to this haven he found in a time of need.

Then, as naked as he entered this world, he exits, walking through the courtyard towards the main street. He struggles walking downhill against the wind, but keeps his head down and treads on, determined. There are no people around and no cars driving by. He moves further, slowly but surely, and as he advances into the distance, he is hardly distinguishable from his surroundings anymore. One would really have to focus to spot the person that keeps moving further, rather than seeing him as part of the buildings, the trees, the cars, or whatever garbage that is blowing in the street. The lack of visibility caused by the weather makes everything blurry and unreal, like an impressionist painting where objects fade into the scenery. He is finally completely absorbed, swept up by the wind and dissolves into thin air; vanishing completely, without a trace while no one is looking.

When Claudio and his son wake up with their collective, monster of a hangover and start wondering where that strange man is - the one who they spent an evening with drinking, who gave them money and left them his bank card - he will already be gone forever; a mythical being that soon enough people will question whether actually existed.

Like a ghost, he will live in people's stories which no one will ever really know whether to take seriously or not. Did he even stay at that inn, or was he only an invention of someone's fertile imagination? Was it all just a big hoax created by some joker? People will keep asking those questions and repeating the story of the man who got swallowed up by the storm, for as long as they meet up drinking in the pub, when they gather around and have nothing interesting to say about their own lives.

ALSO OUT ON FAR WEST

farwestpress.com

+1 (541) FAR-WEST